Clint Faraday Mysteries #18
Dead Low Tide

Two bodies are found on the beach at Los Olivos. People drown in the rip tides there – but these died from the poison of a snake.

That happens, too. The trouble is, the snake is only found in the waters off Australia.

Clint Faraday Mysteries #18
Dead Low Tide
(c)2011 & 2018 by C. D. Moulton

This is a work of fiction. Any resemblances to persons, living or dead, or actual events is purely coincidental unless otherwise stated.

Clint Faraday Mysteries #18
Dead Low Tide

Contents

About the author

CD was born in Lakeland, Florida. His education is in genetics and botany. He has traveled over much of the world, particularly when he was in music as a rock rhythm guitarist with some well-known bands in the late sixties and early seventies. He has worked as a high steel worker and as a longshoreman, clerk, orchidist, bar owner, salvage yard manager and landscaper – among other things.

CD began writing fiction in 1984 and has more than 115 books published as of this time in SciFi, murder, orchid culture and various other fields.

He now resides in Bocas del Toro and David, Panamá, where he continues research into epiphytic plants. He loves the culture of the indigenous people and counts a majority of his closer friends among that group. Several have "adopted" him as their father. He funds those he can afford through the universities where they have all excelled. "The Indios are very intelligent people, they are simply too poor (in material things and money. Culturally, they are very wealthy) to pursue higher education."

CD loves Panamá and the people. He plans to spend the rest of his life in the paradise that is Panamá

- Estrelita Suarez V.

CD is involved in research of natural cancer cure at this time. It has proven effective in all cases, so far. It is based on a plant that has been in use for thousands of years, is safe, available, and cheap. He has studied botany, and was cured of a serious lymphoma with use of the plant, *Ambrosia peruviana*.

Information about this cure is free on the FaceBook page, Ambrosia peruviana for cancer. CD asks only that all who try it please report on its effectiveness on that group.

Dead Low Tide

<u>*Prologue*</u>

Clint Faraday stood on his deck with his fourth cup of coffee to wave at some friends passing in a tour boat, a group of surfers going out to Drago aboard. Silvio waved and went on. Judi Lum, his attractive Oriental nextdoor neighbor came out on her deck and waved, then called that she was going into Bocas Town this morning. Did he need anything? He said, "No. Thanks."

His house phone buzzed. He considered not answering, then went in to see it was a call from a friend, Hank O'Neil, in Puerto Armuelles. The buzzing stopped, so he called the number.

"Clint? Hank O'Neil here, Armuelles. How are things on the Caribbean?"

"Oh, somewhere between merely beautiful and magnificent. How are things there?"

"The weather's beautiful this side. Other things are mostly great.

"I called because some kids were beachcombing at dead low tide and found two bodies washed up on the beach across at Los Olivos. According to Romero, our local supercop, they were murdered. I figured you might be interested."

Clint thought how apt a description that was for when you found murdered bodies on a beach. Dead low tide.

"I'm not doing anything for the past couple of weeks. Is there something that should interest me about this?"

"Well, it's a true mystery. They washed up on a beach,

which generally means drowning. They were killed with some kind of poison or something that Romero says would be called a natural death if they were over there. This poison is from something found only in the waters around parts of Australia. They look like gringos, but he can't be sure until they establish ID. It's likely they're Australian, not gringos, seeing as the poison was from there."

"Could be interesting. I'm not doing anything. I'll come on over to see what's what. I go crazy with nothing to do but lay around and get fat."

"Hah! Fat, you'll never be. You're too much the active type. You can stay in my beach house here. Nobody's here until the end of next month."

"This afternoon. I can leave my boat at Chiriqui Grande, take a bus to David ... I should get there around five thirty or six."

Chapter one

Hank, a big man in his late thirties with a head full of almost shocking red hair, greeted Clint as he got off the bus. He had his Jeep to take them to his place southeast of Puerto Armuelles on the Pacific. It was across from and very close to the wide clean beach at Los Olivos. The day had been perfect, the afternoon very nice. There was a small rain that would get there just before dark, so the night would be a bit cool and pleasant. It could be hot in that area unless there was the usual light breeze coming in off the ocean. The beach house Clint would occupy while there had an almost constant breeze. It was almost low tide, with the tide incoming. The beach was more than a hundred meters wide, now, but would be only six or eight meters at high tide. The tides ran more than fourteen feet here, making for some dangerous rip-tides and undertows.

Hank showed Clint the big refrigerator full of various things and the freezer full of fish, shrimp, conch, etc. He would eat very well indeed! Hank had known Clint for some time. He had stayed at Clint's place in Bocas, and Clint had stayed here before. He had set the automatic coffee pot at six thirty, so there was a full pot waiting. Clint's main addiction, as Hank knew, was coffee.

"We'll talk about the bodies in the morning. I'll take you with me to Romero's and he can give you the basic details. They still haven't been identified.

"If you're not too tired, we can go to the bar for a beer or two. I know the locals will want to say hello and such."

Clint agreed, poured himself a large mug of the excellent

coffee (Panamá coffee is known to be among the world's best) and said he'd clean up and fix a hamburger or something, and would be ready to go. Hank insisted that they would both grab a bite at the bar/restaurant, so just clean up.

They went to the bar at the end of the street by the ocean. Clint knew quite a few of the people there. The gringos frequented the bar, and the word was out that he was there – which meant a number of the local Indios would come. They usually preferred drinking at their own places because of the language and culture differences. Clint spoke Ngobe, but the dialect was different here.

It was a truly great night. He met a girl from Denmark who knew another girl from there who had stayed with Clint a couple of nights in Bocas. She decided she would like to stay with him here, if he was amenable.

He was!

"We'll meet Romero at Yola's for breakfast. The ME, Doctor Geraldo, will be with him. He says this is a very strange thing, but I don't know what he's talking about with all that water snake venom stuff. You might."

Clint agreed. They set off for Yola's place, the popular typical restaurant where the entire staff and most of the early customers knew Clint. They spent the first half hour catching each other up on what was happening here and David and in Bocas, then Dr. Geraldo came in and Clint went with him, Romero, and Hank to a table at the end. Everyone knew that this was a private conversation and left them alone, except to wave when they left for work or whatever.

Clint considered moving to Puerto Armuelles – again.

"I don't know if you're familiar with the water snake off the reef in Australia?" Geraldo began. "It's among the most deadly poisonous snakes in the world. It's found nowhere else, so you can understand why I am perplexed that we have two bodies on the beach here who died from that toxin."

"Yes. *Pelamis platurus*. I've come across it once before in Florida, but simply as a side-issue when we were trying to find what toxin killed a girl. It was considered, at first, but the bite wasn't consistent with the one that killed her, for some reason. I'm surprised you knew about it here."

"The deterioration in the cells and nerves is very distinctive. I found it by working backward on the net, then sent the information to Australia for further confirmation. They sent back the chromatograph signature and it matches."

"Any other marks that would give us any other clues?" Clint asked.

"They were dead for forty five to eighty hours. It's hard to tell, because of the way the poison interferes with natural deterioration processes. A lot of the usual autopsy markers simply couldn't be used."

"Identification is first in importance to me," Romero said. "If we find out who they were, we can possibly find connections to other things."

"I don't know anything except there were two bodies on the beach who died from a rare and specifically locally occurring toxin. This ain't the locally occurring place," Clint replied.

"Yes. One male and one female. Twenty three to perhaps twenty eight years of age. Both had light brown hair and brown eyes. She was five feet six inches, one hundred twenty pounds. He was six feet two inches and one hundred ninety pounds. Both were of slender athletic build. She had a small butterfly tattooed on her left ankle. He had no distinctive marks. Both had perfect teeth that showed they had regular and very good care. They appear to be Europeans, Australians, or gringos. I'm running a DNA match. I believe they will be closely related.

"There's not a lot to go on. The DNA or prints may turn up some answers."

"Is there a good enough record of current flows that you can find the most likely direction they came from?" Clint asked. "We know the time they were deposited on the beach fairly closely. We should be able to locate the area where they were thrown into the water."

"We do?" Hank asked.

"Speed of current, and the direction. They were deposited as the tide went out. We can tell within a few minutes when the tide was at the level where they washed up."

Romero nodded and got up. He said he'd be back in ten minutes (which means at least an hour in Panamá). Dr. Geraldo said it was almost time for him to be in his office, so they'd go there, in a few minutes.

Clint had an idea. He said he wanted to make one short stop, then he'd be there. He went to the malecón (wharf) to talk with two Indio friends fishing there. They knew the local currents and direction better than the "official" records would show. They came from the northwest and flowed to the southeast since the tide change until low tide. They were about six KM/hr more than fifty meters from the shore. Twenty meters from the shore, they were much stronger because the waves caused swells, pauses, and increases.

That meant the bodies came under the malecón or out from it. Coming under it would probably result in being snagged on a piling. They came from outward, moving toward the southeast. They had been in the water for about 35-75 hours or more. At 6KM/hr that was 210 KM or more. That far was in the open Pacific, after the end of the peninsula Puerto Armuelles was on. It wasn't likely bodies came around the peninsula, so they were killed at sea ... but that time would mean tide reversal. Once or twice. 50-105KM. It could have been along the peninsula or just south of the Costa Rica end.

Clint went to the police station and to Romero's office. Romero said the flow was probably about five to eight KM/hr from west to east. Clint said the Indio fishermen said it was six from that direction until they were within fifty meters off the beach.

"The tide was at the level wgere he was found at four twenty, and where she was found at five five," Hank said. "I got that from your friend, Solbiero. He knows that kind of thing better than any records you could find."

Clint nodded. Romero had a call from outside. and went to the records room to return with a printout that said the two bodies were Sandra Moore and her brother, Edwin Moore. They were from New Zealand. She was 24 and he was 26. They were known surfers who had won some competitions. They were from a political family. Lawyers and elected politicians, were moderately popular among their age group, she had been married for three years when her local council member husband was killed in a plane crash while flying back from Sydney, Australia. June 4 of 2009. Passport records showed they had been to several

Latin American and Mexican cities on a surfing tour. They left recently from Acapulco, going to Ecuador. They were on a boat trip. The boat was expected in Ecuador yesterday. It had shown up at dawn today, those two passengers were not aboard. No one knew when they left the boat. It had some minor engine problems and had anchored off of the peninsula that was shared by Costa Rica and Panamá. Romero had a walky-talky to communicate with records as the information was received.

"Well, that certainly makes it our case. They were definitely dumped in our Panamanian coastal waters," Romero declared. "I must contact the captain of that boat and ask that he returns here with all the passengers who were aboard at that stop."

"You can order him to do that?" Hank asked.

"No. I will request that he does. To do so will cause much less of a time delay of their trip than having Ecuador arrest and send them in a month or so, after the usual legal delays and such. The itinerary says they would come here in one week, anyway. It will engender changing the times of the ... a moment! They were to go to Ecuador and stop here as they returned to Nicaragua, where they would cross to the Caribbean side to continue back up the coast, with stops in Cancun and Rotan. Enrique is speaking with Captain Ramos, of Mexico, at this moment. He is saying, yes? ... That the captain is saying it will even be a very good thing. The waves are good here, and there aren't any worth the name in Ecuador, at this time. He is asking his passengers if they would approve of coming back here with the good waves instead of staying where there aren't any. Yes? ... They should arrive here tomorrow between four and five in the afternoon."

"Every once in awhile we do get a break!" Dr. Geraldo said.

"We do that!" Romero agreed. "I will be most happy to accommodate the passengers, who will probably wish accommodations on land after more than a week on the water. I will arrange that with the Hotel Central. This is a slow time of the year here, and they will enjoy having the rooms filled, for a change."

"I don't like this! I don't like it at all!" Clint warned.

"Why..?! What...?" Dr. Geraldo exclaimed.

"If things are going this smoothly, watch for the sudden stop!"

"True," Hank replied.

Chapter two

Clint watched as the passengers came off the gangplank to gather on the big wharf. Ernesto Gevarra, a local guide, would take them to the hotel, the ones who hadn't opted to stay aboard. Some, like the captain, preferred to live aboard at all times possible.

Clint got the captain aside when everyone who was going to the hotel had gone and the others had decided to wander around the town a bit. He would search through whatever records the boat carried on its passengers.

The boat crew was Captain Les Lister ("Lester Lister. I guess my Pa had a weird sense of humor.") and Mate Bob Kelvins. They sailed from San Diego, California, three times per year with these tours. The first stop was Acapulco, then El Salvador, Costa Rica, down to Ecuador, then up to Panamá and Nicaragua, where the tour went across country to go down to the Caribbean side of Panamá and across to Curacao and up through the islands to Miami, from where they went home. The stops here, so far, had been San Diego, Acapulco, El Salvador, Costa Rica (They didn't go to land in Panamá on the way down), Ecuador, and return to Puerto Armuelles.

He handed Clint the passenger information list. He had all their passports in the safe, except when they needed them to go ashore. The arrangement here was that he kept them and gave Romero the list he was giving Clint. If he needed the passports for anything, they could be studied on the boat, unless the holder signed them out and gave them to the police, themselves.

Clint said he might need information from some of them. He didn't know yet.

First was *Sandra Lynne Moore.* Clint had the age and general description already for her and her brother, *Edwin Leigh Moore. New Zealand passports. They'd used them in the USA, Mexico, and El Salvador. They'd stayed aboard for the day and night in Nicaragua, except for three hours at the beach. Not good waves, and the rest were ready to move on.*

Les said the tours were very laid-back, and they made up the itinerary as they went, the majority decision. When there weren't many good waves in a place, they would move on after one day, usually. This trip had found good waves as they passed Panamá. They expected better waves in Ecuador, but that hadn't happened. The group were ready to come back to Panamá for two weeks instead of two days in each of the places there weren't any waves. The tour was popular because of that rule. Fixed tours of two days at each of six beaches where there weren't any waves didn't make for a good time.

Wade James Morrow, 26, New Zealand passport. Canada and the US before boarding.

Cathi Weston Sanders, 24, Sydney, Australia. Canada, and the US before boarding. A note: Trvl w/Morrow. Les explained they were together, but not married.

Martin Marvin Todd, 27, Sydney, Australia. Canada, Mexico, and the US before boarding.

Chester James Vincent, 23, Sydney, Australia. The US before boarding

Ann Marie Sloane-Vincent, 36, Sydney, Australia. The US before boarding. Wife of C. J. Vincent.

Ellen Mae Goode, 22, BC, Canada. The US before

boarding.

Nancy Jean Earle, 23, BC, Canada. The US before boarding.

Janis Rhonda Matheny, 24, Liverpool, England. Australia, Canada, Mexico, and the US before boarding.

Patrick James Matheny, 26, Liverpool, England. Australia, Canada, Mexico, and the US before boarding. Mathenys = brother and sister.

Joseph Ford Perle, 24, Copenhagen, Denmark. Mexico, and the US before boarding.

Lonnie John Johns, 25, Seattle, Washington.

Frederick Donald Derne, 28, New Zealand. Canada, and the US before boarding.

Linda Florence Goodman-Derne, 26, New Zealand. Canada, and the US before boarding. Wife of F. D. Derne.

That was the list. Nothing stuck out very far in that list. Clint felt there were several more likely, marginally, suspects. The obvious were those three from New Zealand. That was so close to Australia that the next on the list would be them. After that, it would be digging for any times of possible contacts before getting on that boat. This was one of those things where the clues would be in that kind of records, most probably.

So! Get to it!

Clint took his copies to the beach house and turned on the computer there. Hank came in to say he would be in Frontera the rest of the day, then to Santiago to help some friends with a land purchase he had vainly tried to keep from ever happening. It was one of those stupid things where they could expect some old Panamanian to show up every year for ten years to claim his or her great grandfather grew a pineapple on the property forty years ago, so they had the ROP – except they would have to get a new plano because the old one was lost. It was a headache situation all the way around, but people won't listen to what they don't want to hear. The land was beautiful, and was what they wanted – and the old man selling it seemed sincere.

He probably was. He couldn't know who would come out of the woods to make a claim.

Clint said it was better you than me. He realized he would get the blame for not warning them.

"I put it in writing, and they signed that they had the information, and it was a personal decision to go ahead with it."

"So?"

He got the finger and a grin with a sigh for that.

Hank drove off. Clint spread the papers he had around to enter several lists that the computer would correlate. That would give him a starting place, at least. As soon as he had something to ask questions about, he would talk with the people involved. He was going to eliminate anyone not from the Australia and New Zealand area, for the time being. Whoever did this had snake venom found nowhere else in the world.

Wade Morrow
Cathi Sanders
Martin Todd
Chester and Ann Vincent
Fred and Linda Derne

Seven on, six off. Unless there was someone who he wasn't considering, for one reason or another. Or something.

First, which of them were the more likely?

He'd concentrate on the unmarried, first. Three.

There is one hell of a lot of information on the web about most of us. It's a matter of finding that one little fact about one person buried in four billion facts about five thousand persons. There were six pages of reference about Wade James Morrow. There were a minimum of eighty four Wade James Morrows. He would have to use another, far more limiting search to find the one he wanted.

An hour later he had it down to six of them. He swore at his stupidity, and went to the boat to get the passport information on the five. While it didn't settle a hell of a lot, it would help to have some information there. Like place of birth, which was on about a third of the sites he was searching.

He got an idea then to add. Trace present ... no good. He had that.

Profession might help, but these three didn't have one listed.

He went back to the comfortable beach house, after a delicious meal at Yola's.

They were surfers. That would limit things a lot, but only if they'd done something noteworthy.

Wade Morrow had used his passport the way Clint already knew. He worked construction for two years and saved the money to spend a year traveling. He was a regular surfer in three spots in Australia and New Zealand. Not in competitions, but planned to do competition surfing after this trip to familiarize himself with conditions elsewhere. Friendly and somewhat gregarious.

Cathi Sanders had been in a number of other countries

before this trip. She was a loner type, but was liked and friendly. She competed in both badminton and volleyball as an amateur. Other countries were Australia, England, Denmark, and France. She could have had contacts with any of the others in the past. Clint noted the dates she was in those countries.

Martin "Marty" Todd was a regular traveler in New Zealand and as far as Hawaii. He had been to California once in the past. Two years ago. Clint noted the dates he was in various places. He was a somewhat known competition surfer, but hadn't won anything not local.

Not much. He got the second list.

Chester "Chet" Vincent and wife Ann.Marie. They went everywhere together. They had been married for three years. Reading between the lines, she paid the bills and he was a personable handsome younger man living off her. There wasn't much to find on the net, except that she had inherited a lot of land and money and a ranch in the outback that made her a few thousand per month. She had met Chet four years ago, while in Sydney on a business trip. She had quite a lot of free time, due to the fact her father had set the ranch up with a system the foreman, a George Miller, controlled. He was good at the job, being the kind who understood that working for a percent was a good thing, so long as he could up the income. He got a sliding percent. The more profit, the higher his percent of the take. She had been married once. Her husband had died in a fire on the outback ranch almost four years ago. He was trapped between two fires that had gotten out of control. They were burning old dry grass for the rains that would come in a couple of weeks. The wind changed, making one of the fires cross the road he could use to escape. He started the fire to the side that would burn toward the road. The one on the other side was burning away from the road. The wind changed. He and another man were caught with no way to escape.

The other married couple from the area were Frederick "Freddy" Derne and wife Linda. They hadn't traveled very much. They both worked in Brunswick, New Zealand. They had saved money to take this trip for three years, since they were married. Freddy was working for a large textile plant where she was the bosses secretary. It was love at first sight. They both liked the water and sailing. Surfing was secondary, but they were both better than average surfers.

Those were the seven on his primary suspect lists. Nothing stuck out. Nobody had a police record beyond a few parking tickets in importance.

So. While he was at it, he might as well look up the others.

Six hours and eight big mugs of coffee later he didn't have a lot, though he had three set aside as needing further investigation. Janis and Patrick Matheny could stand a bit closer look. They had several times been arrested for loud and violent encounters with each other. She accused him of chasing other women, he accused her of chasing other men.

Lonnie Johns was a bit of a brawler. He drank too much and became belligerent, at times. He had a sudden and very violent temper. He was diagnosed as type two bipolar, and seemed to be doing well the past year and a half with stamdard lithium therapy. He understood his problem and would take the lithium when he showed certain signs. He didn't like it, but knew it was necessary if he was going to stop the worst symptoms. He worked for an agricultural company. Deliveries.

That didn't mean a lot – or it could mean everything. Did he have the lithium along, and was he using it?

No one was out of it. Three were the most likely to be involved. Lonnie Johns was least likely for the venom angle.

Clint thought about it a minute longer and brought up Washington, Seattle. There is a serpentarium. Iffy, but well within possibilities.

That was as far as the comp was going to get him with what he had to work on. Time to start meeting the suspects.

Chapter three

El Critico (the popular brothel/restaurante/bar) was fairly busy. Wade Morrow was there, so Clint decided to try him first. He approached him and told him he would have to get some information. It would probably be easier here than sitting in the police station. Morrow agreed. He didn't think he knew anything, but would be more than willing to help, if he could. Murder on a boat he was on was a bit exciting, in a negative way. He knew damned well the murderer was still on that boat.

"Anyone stick out as most likely? Anyone having any kind of argument with the Moores?"

"No. We get along. Any arguments wait until the tour's done. Get into anything serious, and you get dropped off at the next port of call, and you don't get back on. That's part of the deal."

"There doesn't seem to be anyone who would have a motive, from what I've learned," Clint said. "It'll be something from the past, I suppose.

"Did you know them before the tour?"

"We ran across each other a couple of times when the waves were good at a certain place. We had a couple of beers together, once, maybe a year ago, in Point Blanc – that's a sort of popular area for surfers in Australia. I saw the Vincents there, and another place. Marty and I met each other in passing. I may have met Freddy Derne one time, but can't be sure. I never hung out with anybody on this trip before this trip. I didn't have any real likes or dislikes. I've become friends with most of these people. When we're in places like Ecuador was going to be, we tend to party until we can get out. I've made a sort of ... more than friendship, with Nan Earle. We're casual about those things on these tours. Have fun, so long as it's not a problem for anyone else."

Clint nodded. "Does that hold for the married ones?"

"Definitely not. Like I said, so long as its not a problem for anyone. There aren't many swingers on these cruises. Surfers are like that. Have fun 'til you have a wife, then it's over for the fooling around. Of course, that's only on the cruises. I think the Matheny pair would like to swing. They don't, though."

He seemed affable and honest. Clint put him way back as a suspect.

He moved the Matheny pair, as Wade called them, a little more ahead.

He chatted a bit more, then went into town and onto the wharf. Bob Kelvins was sitting there with Cathi Sanders. Clint stopped and asked if they would mind a few questions. Bob shrugged. Cathi said, "Why not?"

"Did you ever notice any friction between the Moores and anyone else?"

"Nothing serious," Bob replied. "They seemed pretty alright. We all liked them. We socialized a bit – me and Marty and Ell and her. Ed and Lonnie hung out a little. They would go with one of the chicks apiece. They hung around a little with Chet and Ann. Sometimes Jan and Pat. Fred and Joe hung out a time or two with Ed. We all get along. Nobody owns anybody, except the chained."

"Jan and Pat did have a few words about him spending time with Ed and Sandy. He told her she didn't have anything to worry about if he was with the two of them. She would have something to worry about if he was only with Sandy, maybe.

"It was more in fun, but I think Jan was a little bit pissed. She wanted to go to a shop in Acapulco, and Pat was on the beach with Ed and Sandy.

"I guess I'm the only broad aboard that knows men do *not* like to shop. That's mostly why Bob and I can get along so good. He understands that women do *not* like football and fast cars."

"Chet and Ann have words, but not with anyone else. She wants to shop, everywhere, all the time, he hates that. She told him once that she ... never mind. It was about looking at some expensive clothes and wigs and shoes. He said that wasn't the kind of things surfers cared about, she said ... never mind."

"That she pays for everything, so he could at least go along with what she likes?" Cathi said. "It's no secret from anyone that he's bought and paid for. He'd very much like to swing, but he knows very fucking damned well he couldn't get away with it for one picosecond!"

"Very short chain?" Clint asked, with a grin.

"Yeah! A choke chain!" Bob agreed.

"No ideas who might have sort of eliminated a nuisance?"

"I heard it was poison?" Cathi asked.

"Yeah. A rare type."

"I suppose I could kill someone, but it would be a knife through the heart. I'm not the girlie type, and poison's a girlie way to kill someone."

Clint laughed. They chatted awhile. Bob was never in it in any serious way. Now she was as much as out of it. She was definitely not the girlie type.

Chet and Ann Vincent moved up. He could think of

several fairly strong motives with their situation. For either of them. Jan and Pat Matheny were up a notch, too.

Speaking of whom, the Vincents were coming out the wharf to the boat. She said she wanted to get a few things to take to the hotel. She wasn't about to stay aboard the boat in port. She liked the services at the hotels that they couldn't get on board. Chet talked with Clint while she went aboard to get her stuff. Clint asked about anything he may have seen or heard, but he said he didn't know much about the others. He'd run across some of them various times, but hadn't developed any friendships. They were somewhat friends with the Dernes. Two married couples, you know. Spending too much time with the singles could lead to problems. They were after different things, and went different places.

"You hang out with the Mathenys any?" Clint asked.

"No." Short and sweet. Chet, at least, didn't like the Mathenys.

Ann came out with a little plastic bag full of cosmetics and a small carry-case with a change of clothes. They strolled back to the hotel, talking about how perfect a place Puerto Armuelles could be.

Clint went back into town and to the bar at the end of the street where the gringos hung out. The Matheny pair and Lonnie and Joe were there. Clint talked with them, but didn't learn anything new. Johns was moved up just a little on his suspect list when he started to gripe about the slow service to a bit of an extreme. He caught himself and said he had a problem, at times. He was bipolar, and would appreciate it if the people he was with would tell him he was going off the deep end. He had medicine that would control it. He could have forgotten to take his medicine and ... but he was the brawler type. You still didn't know how he might react in a given situation.

After a little, Clint could see what Chet felt about Jan. She was somewhat demanding and more than a little spoiled. It was reinforced in a slight subtle psychological way by the upper-class English accents. Clint wondered why they were on the tour, at all.

"You're staying in the hotel?" Clint asked.

"Ha! Not me!" Lonnie said. Joe said he was. The Mathenys definitely were. They could have some luxuries that one couldn't receive on a boat, don't you know, Old Sock.

"Why come on a tour if you don't like the lifestyle on a boat?" Clint asked innocently.

"Oh, just a lark," Pat replied. "The better half likes the surfing, so do I, it was available, we came."

"I've been on other tours, but they were larger vessels," Jan added. "It's not the same – but we are enjoying the adventure, don't you see. No regrets from this side!"

"That does not include a murder or two, thank you!" Pat said. "Other than that, it's been a rather pleasant time."

They chatted some more, then went to their various places for the night.

Clint wanted to know a hell of a lot more about the Matheny pair. They didn't fit with this group.

On the other hand, they didn't *not* fit to much of a degree.

He checked the comp and went to bed. It had been a long day.

In the morning Clint went to the boat to talk awhile with Capt. Les. He admitted that he had preferences among the people aboard, but dared not show it. That would be bad for business.

"What about the English pair?"

"They're a bit stiff, at times, but are alright when they relax. It took a day or so for them to get to know the others, then they were just another part of the group. They all have that kind of mind-set. Surfers will be a little stand-offish for an hour or two sometimes, then they find common interests and things get easier fast. The only one I have to watch this trip is that Johns guy. He has to take medicine or he gets weird and pushy. He tells you that, and asks that anyone who sees him getting to be an asshole, tell him fast, so he can take the medicine. He's been regular, so far. I watch him, but I sorta like him.

"The married ones can be a pain, but that's to be expected. I tried to have a tour for them and another solely for the single ones. It just didn't ever happen. The Mathenys would fit with that. The Dernes fit okay with either. The Vincents are a little hard to figure. It seems like he's a piece of property, sometimes. I guess it's about the age difference. I know my own ideas have changed a little as I got past thirty."

"You tend to mellow out in a lot of ways."

"Yup! I do still like some of the chicks better than the guys, though!"

They chatted awhile, then Clint went back to the police station. Romero was investigating several things, more in the regular police investigation way. He wasn't making much progress in finding who was a killer, but he was eliminating some of them. They compared notes. Not a lot was much different – except Les and Bob were on Romeros list.

"Why?"

"They knew these people before, the Moores. They had been in Cancún twice when both of them were there. Lister and Kelvins say they never met them, but they were there. They could have met them in oh nine or eleven."

Clint nodded. It was certainly a possibility. He considered their personalities, and left them at the bottom of the list of suspects.

All of them had gone to the beach a few miles to the southeast for the surf, so Clint spent his time conversing with people he knew, then went to his beach house computer to spend a couple of hours tracing. He learned very little more – except that the Mathenys were traveling mostly on credit. They did that, and paid everything every February and October. He got his inheritance, a trust, in February, she got hers in October. Both were secure and assured income.

The Vincents had been in some minor trouble in Paris, once. She had accused him of seeing a local prostitute. It turned out she had seen them talking in the park. The prostitute had approached him, and he had declined. Ann had come from a shop just as he turned her down and she had walked off. Ann assumed she was seen coming out of the shop. She started accusing him, loudly enough to attract a police officer. Two old men on the bench a meter away said the woman was a prostitute and had been there long enough for Chet to tell her he wasn't interested. Not two minutes.

It could mean something, but probably not. Everyone on the tour knew that he was bought and paid for, so there wouldn't have been anything there. That didn't eliminate that Ann was jealous of younger women around her property. If it had only been Sandra killed, he would have that one on top of the list.

He moved her up one notch.

He sat back, sighed, and called Judi in Bocas to be filled in on what was happening back home. Things were normal.

He took a cab to the beach at Los Olivos, said to come back for him in an hour, and walked around. There was a stake where the bodies were found, but the tide had been in and out a couple of times since they were found, and there wasn't anything to be seen.

Two Indio children, about eight years old, came to ask if he was there because of the bodies. It turned out they were the ones who found them. They went along the beach at low tide to collect shark's teeth and such the tide brought in. They said everything moved to the east with each tide because the current flowed that way. If there was a very strong rip tide, a lot of things would be brought in. That gave Clint an idea. He strolled down the beach with the kids to where a small deep stream flowed into the Pacific. The tides would push the water up as they rose, then let stuff come back down as they receded.

He went along the stream for a distance, until it got muddy. Going back toward the beach, he found some things in the mangrove roots. They would be deposited there as the tide went out from full. The roots were in the water only for an hour or so at high tide. The distance from where the bodies were found meant the tide would start to rise about the time things from the same time got there. Something could have moved into the stream, which would have only a slight current in, because of the water flowing out – but there hadn't been much rain for the past week or so, so the flow would have let things go quite a distance upstream. If there was anything there, it would be in the muddy section. The Indio kids said he could use their father's cayuca at high tide. Five hours. Dark.

Maybe he would get a good light and take them up on the offer.

They went back to where the taxi was waiting. The driver had a girl with him, so Clint waited a few minutes and made some noise telling the children he'd be back just before high tide. They told him where the house was on the stream, grinned, and pointed with their lips to the taxi. The driver got out of the back seat as soon as he heard them, and the girl got out and waved as she walked toward the road.

Clint went back into Puerto Armuelles and fixed a late lunch, then went into town to buy a powerful flashlight and some extra batteries. The surfers came back at just before five. He greeted them as they got out of the taxis. They said it was a perfect day. The waves were good, if not excellent, and they had a lot of fun.

Clint went home, got into clothes that would take a lot of abuse, and took the taxi of the morning to the neat clean house of the Indios. He was invited inside for some supper, fish, yuca, rice, patacones – delicious. Arturo, the boys' father, took Clint down the stream in the cayuca. Clint searched among the mangrove roots on one side, going down, and on the other, going back up. He found very little. A scarf that was expensive and not the kind of thing sold in the area, some plastic bags, a few cans and bottles, all local types of things.

They went back to the house, where Clint stayed visiting until about ten o'clock, then he called the taxi and went back to Puerto Armuelles, with a set of new friends. The night wasn't wasted, even though he didn't find what he went after. No time is wasted when you meet new friends.

He changed and went to the gringo bar, then to El Critico. He saw a couple of people from the tour, and said hello, but didn't have any questions to ask. He met a woman he'd known for some time and spent the rest of the night at her place.

In the morning he would see what he could find about these people. So far, nothing was pointing to anyone more than others. What he had was a collection of tiny details that were no more than suspicions of vague possibilities. He had nothing specific. He couldn't even find a direction among the group. This wasn't confusing. There wasn't anything to cause any confusion. There wasn't anything. That was the whole of it. He liked a puzzle. There wasn't even a piece of a puzzle to put ... what a mood!

The only physical clue he had was a scarf that could have come from anywhere, and the method of murder. The only reason he considered the scarf as a possibility for a clue was that there wasn't anything else. The poison? If he could find that, it would give him something solid.

No good! The poison had been used. If the killer had more it would be at the bottom of the Pacific, somewhere within two hundred kilometers. Surely, no one would be stupid enough to keep it – unless maybe they planned to use it again. Even that would be inordinately stupid. The killer would surely have gotten rid of any trace of the murder weapon. It would be the only connection with the victims. So. Find another connection.

That would have to wait for morning. Maybe Bob or Les could remember something that would give Clint and

Romero a starting place. The poison used was the only thing that even hinted of a direction. That direction included 7 people immediately, and no one was excluded from the list – except Janis and Patrick Matheny, his prime suspects from a personality standpoint.

Chapter four

Clint went to Yola's for desayuno. Dr. Geraldo was there and they chatted a bit. Nothing new had turned up about the autopsies. The victims were in very good health. They had a slight trace of THC in their bodies, but that would be as much as normal, in their group. Ed had some evidence of having used cocaine a few weeks ago, but it could be from any source. Definitely no regular or repeated use. If there had been bruising, it was close to the injection points, and was deteriorated to the point it couldn't be found.

"There were two injection points on each, about a centimeter apart. Someone tried to make it look like a natural snakebite."

Clint nodded. That gave him another piece of evidence that may or may not mean anything. The killer didn't know the poison was easy to trace to a specific area. That put some of them way down on the list, but most of those were down there, already.

Janis and Patrick Matheny came to knock on his door soon after he returned to the beach house. He was a bit surprised, but invited them in.

"Social call?" he asked.

"Really, we want an idea of who to be careful of on that boat," Pat replied. "We're more than a little bit leery of everyone, now, and that is a most uncomfortable situation. We want to leave the tour, but that copper won't allow anyone to leave the province or county or whatever they call it."

"Surely, you can't possibly suspect Pat or me!" Jan

Page 27

wheedled. "I mean, we are *not* the type of people who commit *murder*!"

Clint bit back his sharp reply, and said, "You are automatically material witnesses. You were there on the boat at the time of the crime, in a limited group. Someone knows something. It could be something they aren't aware they know. How many times before in your life has someone said something, and you said, 'That's right! I hadn't thought of it! It had completely left my mind!' It's something that happens to everyone, at one time or another."

"By Jove, I think you.... You know, that never entered.... It has happened numerous times! By Jove, I think you're right!" Pat exclaimed. "Remember, last Wednesday night, when you said there was some kind of thing missing from what Ann was saying, and you couldn't think of what it must be, Lovey? I said maybe that it was something too much. I never listen to that woman-babble."

"Yes! I said she repeated things in just a little different way to make you think she knows more than she knows! It was about all those fires in Australia. She was there, and her husband, at the time, died, because of one of them. She tries to make it sound like she was fighting the fires – personally, you know. I said, 'She said the fire she was fighting was in one place, then it – it had completely left my excuse for a mind – she had it in another place.' I used almost exactly that expression!

"Very astute of you to think of that. It's very true, in far too many instances. Now I'm a bit concerned that Pat or I may have some little incriminating detail hidden in our minds that could make a *murderer* try to ... Oh, my dear god!"

"That's something the police here and everywhere else are trained to consider," Clint said. "Too many times, the material witness knows something he or she doesn't realize. It can pop into your mind, unexpectedly, at the oddest of times (he was sounding like an Englishman! Knock it off!) and can be the one tiny detail that locks a case up."

"By Jove, that's true!" Pat cried. "Lovey, we are as stupid as people think we are not to have ever even given a moment's notice to the obvious! Of course! That is our value to this sordid affair!

"Mr. Faraday, I have to thank you for hitting me over my hard head with the obvious truth of the matter. I knew it, but it never even ... I'm about to use the expression yet another time! It's something that happens all the time! By Jove, it's true!

"Lovey Dear, we owe Mr. Faraday a debt of gratitude. We think, because we're from a higher station, that they are envious of us here. It's not true! There is a good, solid, certain reason for it!"

Jan was looking shocked, and a little scared. She nodded, and said, "Thank you Mr. Faraday. I do tend to fail to consider things. I'm spoiled a *tiny little* bit by my upbringing, I know. I *do* try to compensate for it. I'm a snob, to put it bluntly. Snobs tend to consider things in the real world from a personal perspective. We miss the facts when we search for explanations. That's because we accept only the explanation that leaves us without blame when things go wrong.

"I *do* know it. I *do* try to stop myself. It is not an intelligent approach to reality."

They chatted a bit more. The two loosened up, and

weren't really so bad as they at first seemed. Still, when they left, Clint thought, *That was weird! It felt rehearsed, but didn't really sound like it was!*

He sat back to think, then went to the computer. Those two were now at the top of his list again. There had to be something, somewhere, to connect them. There wasn't a reason for them to be there at the beach house, except to try to see what the police thought. If there was a lingering question about them, it had to be misdirected. Coming there could well be an attempt to misdirect him.

Would they use that specific poison to try to make it look like it had to be done by an Australian?

Misdirection. They couldn't bring confusion, so were going for misdirection.

He spent four more hours on them, exclusively. Nothing.

He sat back again, poured another cup of coffee, thought, then grinned to himself. "I do it myself, don't I?" he mumbled.

Either the misdirection was going to work, or he had a very big clue to connect someone to something. Question was: Who to what? He knew part of the answer. Maybe "why?" was operative here. He needed the connection between the Moores and the killer.

He went back to the computer keyboard. He started checking on fires in Australia. He also started checking on the dates things happened. There was a contact, but which one?

Maybe "where?" was more important, here. He had to place the Moores, at least one of them, at a specific place at a specific time for this to work as a solution. It wasn't going to be easy, because of having to look at other things to find what he needed and suspected.

One thing was damned certain! The Mathenys were *not* off the top of the list! There could be some kind of secondary set of facts that led to the killings. They could be as much as incidental to something else. Too many of his cases ended up that way.

The way to find this was the boring – and often most critical – part of detective work. More hours on a computer or following people who didn't go anywhere or do anything 99.9% of the time. The computer had reduced the time looking for things that are in records somewhere tremendously. In the "old" days, he would have to communicate through radio or telephone to the location those record were kept. Now he could find them online, in most cases. It was almost entirely a matter of knowing where to look.

The Mathenys were quality people of "station," according to her. That meant a good place to look would be in society pages of the local papers. Wentford Under Bighamton. A small but very expensive area. Matheny.

Okay. Town records first. Matheny, Harold Tristan, was the owner of a large hold he'd purchased from Lord Hittington in 1955. He owned a clothing supply, with connections, at this time, to large Chinese suppliers. Worked mainly through Hong Kong connections. Son, Patrick James Matheny, Second Vice President in charge of international distribution. He hired two secretaries who did the work and reported back to him. Married to Janis Claudette Parker. Her second marriage, but first was annulled after one week because the husband had another wife. Very little note of it. That was because of a small reference that Clint went to court records to find. John Jeffry Jenkins, AKA James Jerold Junger. Newspapers had a short piece on them from time to time, when they attended a fancy function or traveled abroad. They were considered a bit odd, but that was the norm for the age this day and time, eh what?

Three hours. A lot of nothing. They had been to Australia twice, but were mostly at places where they wouldn't be in ... what did Ann's husband raise?

He concentrated on her. Some sheep, some cows, some pigs, some grain crops. The sheep could be wool, which could be a connection.

Awfully slim.

He was on her in Australia, so brought up the husband's story again.

Henry Aaron Fielding. Born August of 1944 – so he was a lot older than Ann. Now she was married to another younger man. She was born in September of 1973. She was 29 years younger than her first husband, and 10 years older than her present one.

Very successful outback rancher. Some friction with neighbors when he went into sheep herding, but he fenced and kept them in the interior of his land. Active in social causes in a lukewarm way. Very strongly the "Australia for Australians" mentality. Adamantly against government subsidies for foreigners starting businesses that took jobs and commerce away from natives. Give welfare to Australians, only, and those must have a real and immediate need. Don't pay bums to be bums.

There wasn't much about the fire, except in local records. Those made terse and succinct into an art form. There was a fire, he got trapped by a wind shift, his funeral was two days later. In other news....

Another day of thousands of details about all of them,

with nothing new. No one's position on his list was changed. He sighed heavily and went out on the porch with the sea view. It was almost five, and he was dead tired. Actually doing something physical didn't tire him. This did.

Wade Morrow was walking along the beach. He spotted Clint, and waved, then came toward him. They exchanged greetings, and Clint invited him in for a cold beer. They sat on the porch in silence for about five minutes, then Wade said, "Clint, I think there's some kind of suspicion in the back of my mind about someone, but don't want to repeat what's probably only rumor – but it could be important. It's something I saw in Acapulco when we were getting on the boat."

"I guarantee confidentiality. Always. I won't do or say anything if it leads nowhere, and probably not, if it does."

"Well, there was a paper Sandra had that she picked up at the marina. It was one of those silly scandal things Murdock or somebody prints. It had a story about a company that Sandy had folded to read. I thought it was a little strange. Something about some person who died at a very convenient time, or something. He had a mistress, and the wife found out, then he had an accident. I wouldn't have noticed, but Ed, Sandy, and I were just walking up the ramp together, and she showed it to Ed. He said it wouldn't surprise him. It was something that happened a hell of a lot too often, anymore. He damned well wouldn't put it past her.

"We went inside, and I didn't think much about it, at the time. I think it could mean that they read something about someone and it connected, for some reason. That they knew the person or he wouldn't have said that in the same way. You know what I'm saying?"

"He sounded like he knew her, and wouldn't be a bit surprised if she knocked over a cheating husband."

"Exactly."

"I have to check on another person. It's someone I've had a lot of suspicion about. It would give me motive, which is more than I have now. If she's the only one with motive, it'll likely be her."

They chatted awhile. Wade said he'd see Clint later, and left. Clint went to the computer. What was the name of Janis's two week husband?

J. J. J. Two. He checked. He had done that once before, married a woman when he already had a wife. He was after the money. He married into it.

Bingo? He died in a hit-and-run accident in Manchester, nine days after his annulment. One thing was certain, now! Clint was going to do a thing he very rarely did. He was going to concentrate on one suspect. That could be a big mistake, but he didn't see anyone else viable.

Still, it seemed too pat.

He sat back to think, then went back to the computer to check the scandal sheet newspapers for stories about them. He checked all of them, while he was at it. He didn't want to overlook one thing because he thought he had found something else.

Uh-oh! Cathi Sanders was living with a man for a couple of months when he fell off a fourth floor balcony onto a concrete sidewalk and died. He was drunk, at the time. Cathi wasn't in the apartment when it happened, so far as they knew. She said they were getting along pretty well, and were contemplating marriage, but neighbors said that wasn't entirely true. They had been overheard a couple of times when they got into loud and vulgar arguments.

Both Ellen Goode and Nancy Earle were at a tournament where George B. Hopkins drowned when he was surfing, alone, early in the morning off of Baja California. The waves were high, and it wasn't uncommon for some competitors to practice alone, though it wasn't common practice, either. It was known to be dangerous.

Clint brought up the autopsy report through the police site he had the codes to enter. It seemed a normal drowning. There was a large contusion over his right eye. It was assumed he flipped, and the board caught him over the eye, knocking him unconscious. He died of drowning.

Crap! Did all of them have a dead body in their past?

He didn't find anymore evidence of any such thing.

He sat back to think. A small grin lit his face for a few seconds, then he got up, showered, and went into Puerto Armuelles. He saw several of the group, then went onto the wharf to talk with Les, who knew nothing more. He then said he'd like a word with Bob, but he was with a girl in town. Clint said it would wait until morning.

Chapter five

Clint had his coffee at home, then went into town for more at the hotel café, then went to the wharf. Bob was just coming onto the wharf from his night in town, and they walked together to the boat.

"Bob, I need to know a little about a couple of the people on the boat that's not such common knowledge. It seems there's a body or two in more than one of their pasts. I'll ask about more than I'm concentrating on. Don't make any hasty conclusions about it, Okay?"

"Yeah. Fine with me."

"Frederick Derne. Does he always get along with everyone, or does he get weird, once in a while?"

"He's just a little out of place, but not weird. I've never seen or heard anything, except for when Linda wants to go some places he doesn't, and vice versa. They work it out."

"Nan Earle?"

"Just a surfer girl. Her and Ell sort of hang out, now and then."

"Marty?"

"Sort of hard to figure, sometimes. Wants to more or less be a loner. Better surfer than he lets on. Never had a problem of any type."

"Cathi?"

"Surfer girl. Has a temper, sometimes, but takes it out on things. She gets really upset about guys who hit on her and won't take no for an answer, but she'll break something. She won't do more than cut the stupid creeps down. With words, you know."

"Ann Vincent?"

"Hard to like. She's possessive, when there's no reason to be. Chet knows which side of the bread the butter's on. You can't ask about one of them without getting answers about both of them."

"Janis Matheny?"

"Spoiled and a snob, but she admits it, and we all get along. It's that overdone British accent that puts you off. They're pretty good people, after you get to know them. She says to tell her to piss off when she goes too far. She has a tendency to give orders. We've all told her to piss off. She just laughs, and says, 'Thank you!' She really means well. It's all in how she was raised. A rich only child. She says that. She tries hard to be a regular person."

"Sandy Moore?"

"She's dead ... I see. What did she do or say to set someone off?

"She was a lot of fun. So was he. They didn't make judgments, usually. She didn't like Ann much, because Ann was always so suspicious. She said that Chet was a kept man, and that took any possibility of anything 'way off the table. She and Janis made an effort to get along, and it worked. They started off not liking each other much – sort of competition. Sandy was goodlooking as hell. When Jan learned she wasn't about to get involved with any married man, they became sort of buddies.

"I don't know if you know the surfer crowd very well. They can turn from cold to friends in a day. They get to know each other and where they stand. The only pecking order is in the tournaments. Outside of that, they're equal, unless they do something to make them unequal."

"Joe is the only other one I need to know anything about. I've talked with Wade, and he's another one who admits he has problems and tries to overcome them. He doesn't get pissed when you tell him he's out of line. He knows it."

"Joe? Another one who's hard to get close to. He's just a regular type guy. Gets competitive at tournaments, but keeps it there. Quiet, but a more serious type.

"Any help?"

"It makes most of what I felt a little more clear. Thanks."

They talked about the waves for a couple more minutes. Clint went on out the wharf to talk with Indio friends who were fishing there.

"Silvio, have you noticed anything about any of the people on the surfer boat?"

"Anything? No. Those two gringas are hot, but they stay with their group."

"I just need some basic background. They seem normal enough, to me."

He grinned. "For surfers, I guess so."

"I saw something a little strange about one of them," Berto said. "One of the women. I was underneath, and didn't see which one. She threw some things in the water."

"In the water ... things?"

"Bottles."

"Where?"

"Just by the tie-down on the end. I was on the painting scaffold, and she came out, about ten last night, and threw them in. I think it was one of them. It could have been someone else. She left back toward town. She was too tall for a Panameña, and walked too heavy. Many gringas walk heavy. I saw her hair was a little short for a Panameña. Sort of brown. I couldn't see much else."

"What kind of dress? What color?"

"Just those blue pants that fit so tight."

"Wet suit?"

"Yes."

"Are you certain it was a woman?"

"Women's shoes. I couldn't see much of her from underneath, but those shoes are stupid on a wooden dock. She almost fell when she stepped in a crack."

"No one else was on the wharf? None of the local fishermen?"

"Tide was wrong. No fish. Nobody else I saw."

Clint nodded and thanked them. He went to the beach house and got the scuba gear from the closet, checked the air and regulators, then went back to the wharf and down to the landing station under the control house. He put on the gear and slipped into the water to go underneath to the area where the bottles had been thrown in. It was in sixty two feet of water, so he wasn't seen by anyone.

He found various odd things there. Four were fancy expensive cosmetics dispensers. He put everything there in a sack and went back to the landing and off of the wharf with his loot. He took everything to Dr. Geraldo, and said he wanted to know everything they could find about what had been in those containers.

"Like, was it snake venom?"

"Uh-huh."

"Two hours. It's not a fast test to find that kind of specific in trace amounts."

"Will do!"

Clint went back into town, where he wandered around while he waited. The group had gone out surfing again, and wouldn't be back before five or five thirty. The waves were still good. A little better than yesterday and the day before.

Not much else to do, so he visited friends in the nearby countryside and returned to town at four thirty, Dr. Geraldo said most of the tests were inconclusive, but he got a probable confirmation from a cologne sprayer bottle. It was expensive.

"Which one?"

"The Arpage Musk. Real gold leaf logo, and all that."

"Sounds like we have one small physical clue! Good show!"

"If you can find who it belonged to."

"There is that."

"I have a partial. It's not enough for positive, unless we can match it in portion to a full print. It's not a thumb or first, so it's not on passports or tourist papers."

Clint nodded. He and Geraldo went to the hotel bar for a beer and waited until the group got back. The taxi let some off at the wharf before coming to the hotel. They greeted them all as they came in. Wade came over to have a beer with them. They chatted about whatever came up.

Clint liked all of them. He knew one was a killer, but that didn't make them less likable, in other ways. They were all going to a shindig some other local surfers they met were throwing. The others lived in the area, and had been there on the beach for the good waves today. They all got along. One of them, San Diego Tom, had met three of the party in Sydney, at a tournament in Australia send-off. Two years ago.

Clint had met San Diego Tom several times. People here were called by a specific name like San Diego Tom because there were a number of Toms in the area, so that designated which one you were talking about. There was an El Paso Tom and an Old Tom in the area that Clint had met. There was a local, Tomas Carenas, they called by his family name. Carenas.

That might tell him something. He had something he wanted to know that a semi-dress-up shindig might tell him.

Wade invited him. "San Diego Tom told us he knew you from when you solved some kind of mining case. He said the Indios considered you one of them. He said to tell you to join us. You somehow fit with about any group."

"I'm Ngobe. These are different, but we're still Indos."

"You're shitting me! *You*, an Indio?!"

"So declared by two chiefs," Geraldo agreed. "If they declare you're Indio, you're an Indio. I suppose you might call him a naturalized Indio."

They chatted, then Clint went to the beach house to get ready. He just might get a small clue as to who to grab. He only had one serious candidate, now. Somebody not being somewhere and somebody else doing the wrong thing in getting rid of those containers in that strange manner. That little deal told him someone knew.

Tom saw Clint come in with Wade, and came over to greet him and ask him if there was any progress in the case. Clint said it was pretty well in the final moments, that he just had to get confirmation about something. Several of them heard that, and looked expectant. One of them just hid a quick smirk, but Clint saw it. It confirmed what he thought. Another looked scared and a little relieved.

"Well, let's have a drink or ten and forget about that stuff for the night!" he said. "Everybody who doesn't know, which is no one, this is Clint. Eat drink and be merry! Tomorrow we diet!"

That was his favorite saying. He was constantly fighting a middle-age bulge. He had just turned fifty five a couple of weeks ago, but was still a regular surfer. He had won a few trophies in the past, and was determined to surf until he died, preferably crushed by the really ultimate wave.

Chapter six

Clint had about all he needed, except who the woman was on the wharf. He had an idea. Some things were beginning to click, now. Some people were in very bad situations because of what they didn't know. Maybe someone found a way out.

A few other things were adding up. He went back through what he'd learned, step-by-step, and it was there. That perfume bottle made it fairly clear who it was. Things told him not so long ago fell into place when Berto was describing the woman on the wharf. Someone wanted out of what had become an intolerable situation. Someone who was the only one there with access to a perfume bottle. He had said, when they were looking for a container for the venom, that the person who brought it would be a fool to keep it or dispose of it where a killer could be connected. Someone else used that.

Clint decided to go calling. He needed a little information from one person to tie this up.

"Hi, Wade. How are things today?"

Clint was just going into the hotel as the group was loading their gear into the taxi to go to the surfing beach. San Diego Tom was with them. He said the waves were as good as they got this time of year, today, and he wanted to take advantage of them.

"Surfing is one of those few things you don't do, right?" Wade asked.

"I'm lousy at it, and am too old to learn," Clint said. "I hang four when I need to hang ten. A board can give you a hell of a smack if you don't know how to fall where it can't. I don't. Any real surfer has that as an automatic."

"Something you don't even think about," Tom agreed. "Want to come along and watch?"

That wasn't what he'd planned, but might make this a bit easier. "Why not?"

He got in the back of the small truck taxi with Wade, Joe, and the gear. Half of them were in the second taxi. They made the trip to the beach, where they unloaded the gear, scanned the waves, and said they were almost perfect, and would be perfect in about an hour and a half. The tide would change and start coming in in a few minutes. It was dead low tide, at the moment.

Cathi came with Bob and the Dernes to chat a few minutes until the Vincents and Ell and Nan came to get their boards. The Mathenys stayed mostly off to themselves. Lonnie and Joe were talking with Wade and Marty.

Ann said she didn't care to take to the water yet. Her back was giving her some trouble. She'd slipped and twisted her ankle on the sidewalk, and it had now settled to her lower back. Nan said, "Sciatic nerve got pinched. I'll give you a quick massage."

They took a roll-out mat to halfway to the water where Ann laid down for the massage. It was a good opportunity, so Clint called Chet to the side for a few questions.

"I need to know a few odd things before we arrest Ann for the murders," he began. "I really only need answers for personal reasons. We have her cold for the venom. Thanks for that."

He looked scared. He stared at Clint, and waited.

"You don't make a good drag, but it served pretty well for an Indio under the wharf to think it was a gringa. Did you wait until you knew he was under there and no one else was at the dock, or was it just good luck?"

"I waited. It had to work or nothing ever would, and she'd kill me off, sooner or later."

"She was purely stupid not to get rid of that bottle when she dumped them overboard."

"She did throw it out. It floated enough that I got it in a hand net when she went back inside."

"She killed her last husband?"

"I think so. I don't know. I didn't know anything about any of it until I saw her push Sandy over the side. I was supposed to be asleep. I think she put something in my beer before we went to bed. It was a powder that tasted bitter. I saw her do something, and acted like I drank the beer and dumped it when she went to the head. I didn't know what was going on, and pretended to get sleepy, so we went to bed. I acted like I was out, and she left the room and was gone about an hour when I went to look for her.

"She was on deck, pushing Sandy over the side at the gangplank break. I stayed in the doorway, and she went to their room and came back with some things. The bottle was one of them. She dumped them, and went back to their room. I fished the bottle up and went back to our room. She came in about five minutes later and I acted like I was out cold. I know what that stuff can do, so I kept saying my head was a little painful the next morning, and I couldn't think straight.

"I was scared nearly out of my mind! I didn't know what to do, and she got to where I couldn't be alone for ten seconds or with anyone else where she couldn't hear. Everyone said you had a knack for digging things up. I know you're watching all of us, and that the Indios will tell you anything they know, no matter what.

"I also knew there was no one else with that expensive perfume on board. I didn't know for sure, but that would be the perfect way to carry snake venom where it would be hard to find. I didn't touch that bottle. I used latex gloves. Her prints would be on it, and you'd tag her. All I had to do was make it look like she dumped it somewhere and you found it.

"I gave her some stuff for her back. She did slip, and did strain it a little. She magnifies a little pain into a major operation, so she took it, and I knew she would be out for four hours. The pain and headache this morning would be a natural reaction, and she wouldn't be suspicious.

"I waited until I saw the Indio go under the wharf and went home to get the bottle and a wig and shoes that would make it look and sound like a woman from underneath and ... you know the rest."

"There weren't any fingerprints we could use, but the bottle tells the story. It had a little of the venom in it. It could only be her perfume on that boat."

"She thinks there's no way you'll ever find anything about whoever did it. She says she thinks it was someone smart as all hell who didn't leave any clues anywhere. She was glad there wasn't any connection to us, because that would make you suspicious."

"What was it about? Do you know?"

"I can sort of guess it had something to do with something in a used magazine Sandy bought in Acapulco. She said she was sure it would cause someone a whole lot of trouble. They would have grounds for one hell of a lawsuit for libel.

"She got Ann aside and she and Ed were sort of intense when they were talking to her. Ann said they found something about someone in the magazine, but it was probably not the one she thought, but they would look into it. Sandy said something about something else that made the connection pretty sure. They went into Ed's room for awhile, then Ann came back and said it was a big disappointment. The person's age in the magazine said fifty four, and nobody on this trip is that old, except Les, and it sure as hell couldn't be about him."

"I've seen Ann about ten times here," Clint said. "She always has on a different wig. She has a wig on now, and she's going surfing. What's that about?"

"She has a little patch of hair missing. She got a burn in one of those fires in Australia. It was just a few days before her husband died in one of them. She's sensitive about it. She kept talking about having a graft when we were in Paris. She said nobody'd ever know, and she wouldn't be so embarrassed about it."

"Funny. There's no record of her being injured in a fire."

"It was in the outback. She put some antibiotic salve on it and hoped it wouldn't scar to where it would show."

"I see. That's what it would be about. I'll have to find a copy of that magazine, but it will be something that shows she killed her husband. Maybe the missing hair patch is some kind of proof of identification."

"I sort of thought something like that. I would have turned her in at Acapulco, but she could kill me without a thought, I think. If she finds out about this, she will, anyhow."

"Exactly where were you when this happened? Do you know fairly close? I can make it look like something else."

"We were sitting at five kilometers off the point light. We could see it, and Les said we wouldn't have to go through a lot of silly rigamarole with officials if we stayed a ways out of Costa Rican or Panamanian water for the night. A patrol boat did come close, but we were past the limit, and they went on."

"What time?"

"It was three twenty seven when I got back to my room. I made sure I remembered that."

"That's all I need!" Clint said. "She'll look this way in a minute, so don't be talking to me."

He nodded and went to stand just behind the taxi, polishing his surfboard. Ann came up the beach to Clint about three minutes later and said she thought he was going to talk to Chet. She seemed a little unduly suspicious. Clint said all he wanted to know was if he'd seen a girl called Surfer Sally in Ecuador, but Chet said they didn't stay long enough to meet anyone. That seemed to satisfy her. She went to tell Chet that she was perfect, now! All she needed was to make the muscle against her spine where the sciatic nerve went in relaxed. They could catch the waves, now, but she mustn't twist too much. They went down the beach with their boards.

The taxi was returning to Puerto Armuelles. Clint called a farewell to the group and went with it. In Puerto Armuelles Clint went directly to the police station and had a chat with Dr. Geraldo and Romero. Romero said he'd get an evidence bag from the Costa Rican police and make out a report that made some very interesting facts known. Clint said it would wait until they were all back. They made a plan. Clint went to the boat and told Les what they needed, so he said he'd manage to have them all on the wharf for a party and luau-type feast at nightfall. It was one of the things that were advertised as part of the tour. Surprise Hawaiian luaus when they found good waves. They wouldn't think much about it not being on the beach, because that was a bit far. He had time to get things ready, and had done that sort of thing before. If Clint would get some friends to bring a lot of beach sand onto the dock fast enough, he'd get the cooking started. It would take eight hours, which meant it would be ready about six thirty.

Clint had several of the Indios start bringing sand and some rocks, plus a lot of old tree limbs the electric company had cut along the streets last week. Les said they would make the fire about right for the rock-bed.

Clint went back to the police station when the process was well underway where he helped Romero compose the report that came into the station half an hour ago, along with the bottle.

Then Clint went back to the beach house to relax and take care of his other business on the computer.

Judi and their weird musician/botanist/author friend were there to surprise him. Judi had an idea she would try, and Dave would be there to supply music for the luau. Clint called Romero and told him what Judi planned. None of these people had ever seen her, and she could pull it off. It would make it just a tad bit more legitimate sounding.

The fest was just starting. Everyone was relaxed and having fun. Wade and Joe had invited a couple of local girls, and Ell had made friends with Silvio, Clint's Indio friend. Dave was doing some older songs everyone knew, and they were singing along to *Leaving On a Jet Plane* when Romero, Dr. Geraldo, and Judi came out on the wharf. Nobody was paying them any attention until Dr. Geraldo announced, "This is Judi Lum, a liaison with the Costa Rican police. She has brought us some things that were picked up by the Tica patrol boat at the point. We told them of the deaths, naturally, because we weren't altogether positive it was in Panamanian waters or Costa Rican waters or international. They saw and recorded that this boat was sitting off the point only meters outside the limit. They note all such things.

"When we informed them of the murders, they immediately dispatched a vessel to that spot. The loran numbers were, of course, noted when the report about the presence of the boat was entered. The waters there are but six to fourteen meters deep at low tides, making a scuba team search quite easy.

"They found something. A perfume bottle. It was for a very expensive perfume. Miss Lum has brought it and the report (he waved some legal-looking papers) to me at just before noon." Judi had a stern look. She nodded, and said, "We have now authenticated this find, as well as such type of evidence can be authenticated. The chain of evidence is unbroken from the finding of that evidence to this moment. It will remain unbroken. It is damning evidence against which no one can escape.

"Continue, please, Dr. Geraldo. I will not interrupt again, unless it becomes necessary."

"The police know how to handle what may be evidence. The bottle had not been touched, except with tongs to place it into the evidence container. As I am equipped for study of evidence better than are they I would perform various tests, though they found a fingerprint on the bottle. (Ann gasped).

"I found venom of a water snake found only in certain restricted Australian waters. It is a unique toxin. It is easy to trace, if one knows what to look for. I was engaged in looking for exactly that poison produced by *Pelamis platurus* at the time. It was found in trace amounts inside that bottle. Combined with the fact that only one of you would use that perfume – only one of you – and that one with a matching print, well you know the obvious conclusion that must be reached."

Ann sank down to the wharf and groaned.

"Would you care to tell me why?" Romero asked.

"She found an article in a magazine that said I was suspected of killing my husband. I could claim I wasn't the one it referred to, except the reporter had a picture of me that was taken when I was changing wigs. It was taken on a hotel surveillance camera, and showed the patch of missing hair I got at that fire. I've been traveling since. The Australian police will be very quiet about it until I'm back in their jurisdiction, then will arrest me. I hoped to be able to have a graft that would hide the spot, but there was never a place I could do it.

"I went to a doctor in Acapulco. He said he could do the operation for ten thousand dollars. I was to leave the tour at Nicaragua on a pretense, and go there.

"Sandy found the article, and said the picture looked just like me. She and Ed were together. I said it definitely wasn't me, although my husband did die in a fire, and the picture looked like me, in some ways. I wore wigs because of chemotherapy that left several patches of hair that never grew back. It would be easy to show them the patches weren't at all like that picture, and that it was easy to tell when hair just fell out from the chemo and when it wasn't growing on a scar.

"We agreed that I would do that, but I said I was humiliated enough that anyone would think I would kill anyone. I would show them my hair loss in private.

"Ed was with Bob and Ell, so we agreed that I would come to their room when he went back. I got things together – I carried the venom because ... because you never know when you might need something like that. I never realized you could trace venom to the exact snake. When I learned that, I knew I'd be caught, unless I could direct attention elsewhere. I thought I had. I hadn't. It's all over.

"I do love you, Chet. I would never ever do anything to hurt you. Ever. Did you know about my husband?"

"No. I suspected there was something, but I didn't know what it was."

"Well, I'm afraid you'll have to come with me," Romero said. "It's a sad affair."

She stood up, sighed, then suddenly ran to the edge of the wharf, but Judi grabbed her before she got there.

"Not this time. They'll just send you back to Australia so they won't have to go to the expense of housing you for the next twenty years, then send you back," Judi said. "Clint always arranges that sort of thing. Panamá has enough to pay for without millions of dollars for foreigners to be incarcerated. We don't want to be bothered in Costa Rica, either. (She rolled her eyes at Clint where the others couldn't see. She had almost forgotten she was supposed to be from Costa Rica.)"

"Okay. It was stupid. I would end up in the water, and

I'm a good swimmer. I just didn't think."

"Romero, why not arrange for her deportation to Australia and arrest her in the morning?" Clint asked. "She can't go anywhere here. Might as well stay at the party and at the hotel at her own expense tonight. It's all out in the open, so maybe the rest of us can have a good night."

"You're a really decent person, aren't you?" she asked. "I won't run anymore. It's almost a relief to know I won't have to anymore. Maybe I'll enjoy the party, too."

It turned into a good night.

"Well, back to Bocas, I guess," Judi said. "It's been a very good week. I really do like Puerto Armuelles."

"I liked it so much I moved here," Hank, who had returned the day before, said. "It's too quiet for a lot of people, but it's a good place to be."

"I was surprised at how that bunch accepted Ann so much better after they knew than they did before," Judi said. "She was here, not even arrested, for almost two days. Chet turned out to be a nice enough guy. I'll bet he never marries for a free ride again!"

"Surfers are like that," Dave said. "You don't try to hide something, and they'll get along. Wade and Marty spent a lot of their time at El Critico. Ell and Nan are fun people. Regular surfer girls. All of them like to party."

"Well, they're going to stay the final week here, then finish the tour. Ann insisted that Chet stay with them. She said she had him so cornered for so long she's surprised *he* didn't kill *her*! She just didn't know what else to do. She was on the run, and no one there knew it. She was acting like a fool. She was terrified he'd find another woman," Clint noted. "She talked with me for a couple of hours. Unloading.

"Her first husband was for money and station, so she couldn't fault Chet for doing the same thing to her. She's going to try to file a self-defense rendering in court. Her first husband did beat her up, once, but it was because he caught her with another much younger man. It won't float.

"I suppose I ought to go back to Bocas, but there'll be something else. I'm getting lazy."

"I'm going back to Cusapín for a week or so. Come along," Dave suggested.

Clint thought about it. It sounded good to him!

"Okay. Coming along, Jude?"

"Why not? It's the only place I like on the order of here and Bocas."

"There's always David," Hank suggested.

"It's a city. I'm getting spoiled ... but it's not like a city. It's a big city that's like a puebla."

They chatted awhile, then decided to decide where to go tomorrow.

C. D. Moulton's works are available on most major outlets as printed or e-books. CD writes the CD Grimes, PI mysteries, the Det. Lt. Nick Storie mysteries, the Clint Faraday mysteries, the Flight of the Maita science fiction series, books on orchid culture and many others of many types. Mystery, adventure, intrigue, science fiction, fantasy, para-normal, mild erotica, and factual.